USBORNE FIRST NATURE BOOKS

FLOWERS

Wen ... rgess ·
Mic ... nney ·

Vict ... tons) ·

C ... art ·

Published in the U.S.A.
by Hayes Books, 4235 South Memorial Drive, Tulsa, Oklahoma, U.S.A.

USBORNE FIRST NATURE
FLOWERS

ROSAMUND KIDMAN COX
and **BARBARA CORK**

Designed by **DAVID BENNETT**

Games in this book

1. Hunt the Bumblebee

Bumblebees visit flowers. Can you find 20 more Bumblebees in this book ?

2. Watch the flower open

Hold the book like this.

Watch the top right hand corner and flick the pages over fast.

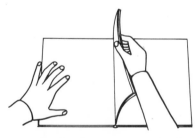

watch here

Looking at Buttercup flowers

If you look closely at a flower, you will see that it is made of lots of different parts.

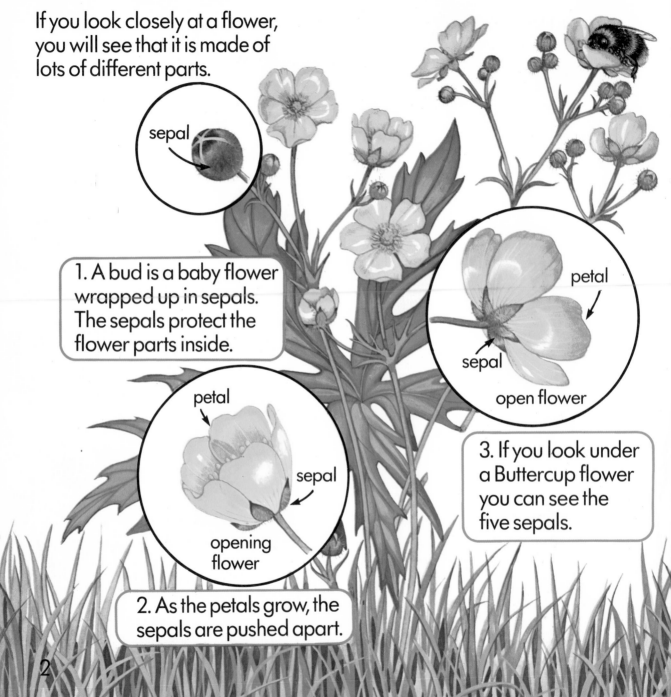

sepal

1. A bud is a baby flower wrapped up in sepals. The sepals protect the flower parts inside.

petal

sepal

open flower

petal

sepal

opening flower

2. As the petals grow, the sepals are pushed apart.

3. If you look under a Buttercup flower you can see the five sepals.

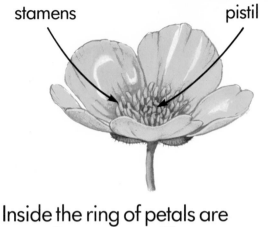

stamens   pistil

stamens

pistil

Inside the ring of petals are more flower parts. The green parts in the centre are called the pistil. Around it are stamens.

If you pull off the petals and sepals, you can see all the parts inside.

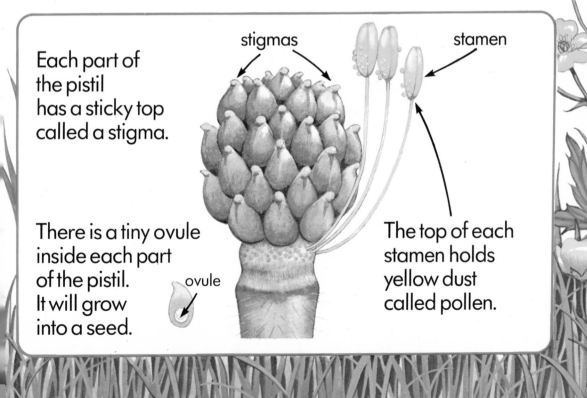

stigmas   stamen

Each part of the pistil has a sticky top called a stigma.

There is a tiny ovule inside each part of the pistil. It will grow into a seed.

ovule

The top of each stamen holds yellow dust called pollen.

Looking at flower parts

Flower parts can be different shapes and sizes and different colours. You will have to look closely at each flower to see which part is which.

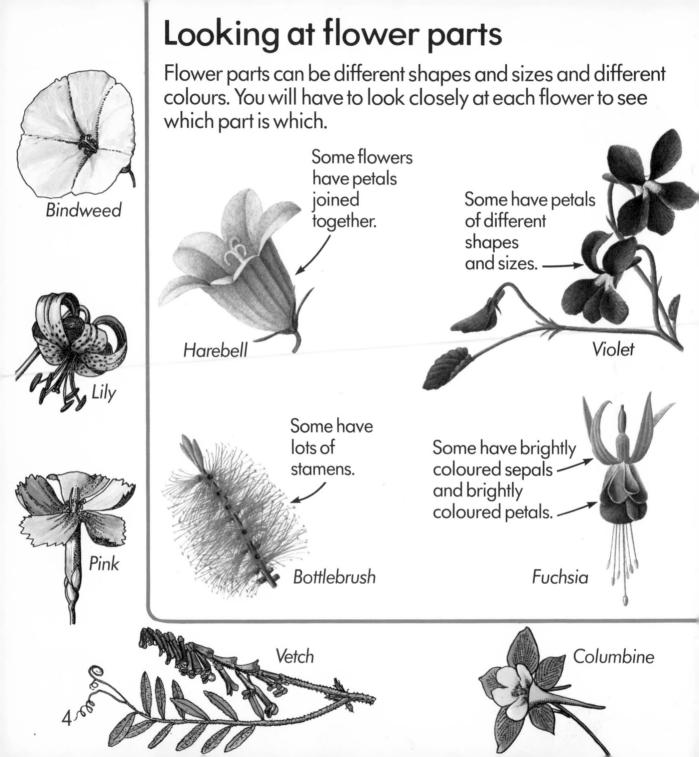

Bindweed

Lily

Pink

Some flowers have petals joined together.

Harebell

Some have petals of different shapes and sizes.

Violet

Some have lots of stamens.

Bottlebrush

Some have brightly coloured sepals and brightly coloured petals.

Fuchsia

Vetch

Columbine

4

Some flowers have a pistil with only one stigma.

Crocus

Daffodil

Some have a pistil with more than one stigma.

Cranesbill

An Aster flower is made of lots of tiny flowers.

An Aster has tiny flowers on the outside with one long petal.

If you pull an Aster to bits, you can see the tiny yellow flowers on the inside.

The Bumblebee is somewhere on this page.
Do you know why he visits flowers?
The answer is on the next page.

Daisy

Dandelion

Dahlia

5

The visitors

Cranesbill

Flowers have many visitors. They are usually insects, such as bees.
The Bumblebee visits flowers to drink a sweet liquid called nectar.
Sometimes the visitors eat some of the pollen.

Yellow Flag

Visitors to this flower
need long tongues to
reach down to the nectar.

Many flowers have
guide-lines or dots
that point the way
to the nectar.

Nectar is
in here.

6

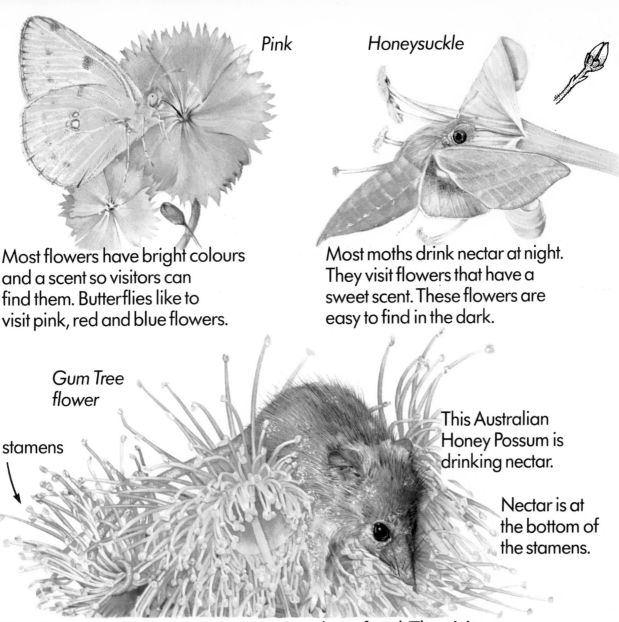

Pink

Honeysuckle

Most flowers have bright colours and a scent so visitors can find them. Butterflies like to visit pink, red and blue flowers.

Most moths drink nectar at night. They visit flowers that have a sweet scent. These flowers are easy to find in the dark.

Gum Tree flower

stamens

This Australian Honey Possum is drinking nectar.

Nectar is at the bottom of the stamens.

The flowers help the visitors by giving them food. The visitors also help the flowers. Do you know what the visitors do? The answer is on the next page.

Why flowers need visitors

Visitors help plants by moving pollen from flower to flower.

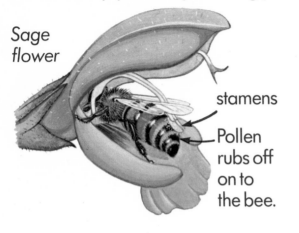

Sage flower

stamens

Pollen rubs off on to the bee.

pollen

1. As a bee collects nectar from a flower, its body gets covered with pollen.

2. It flies to another Sage flower. It has pollen from the first flower on its back.

stigma

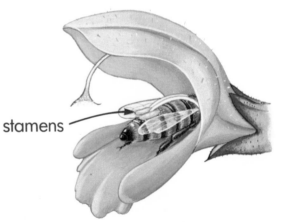

stamens

3. As it lands, the pollen on the bee's body rubs on to the stigma of the flower.

4. The bee goes into the flower. New pollen from the stamens rubs on to its back.

8

Fuchsia

Hummingbird

The Hummingbird is drinking nectar from a Fuchsia flower. It has some pollen from another Fuchsia flower on its breast feathers. As the bird drinks nectar, the pollen on its feathers rubs on to the stigma of this Fuchsia flower.

Watching for visitors

Find a flower that has stamens and a stigma that are easy to see. When the sun is out, sit down and wait for the insects to come.

Tulip

When the insect flies away, look to see if it has left any pollen on the stigma of your flower.

If an insect comes, try to see if it has any pollen on its body.

9

How the wind helps flowers

The flowers on this page do not need visitors to move their pollen. The wind blows their pollen from flower to flower.

Plantain flowers

False Oat Grass flowers

These flowers have no scent or coloured petals to attract visitors.

Plantain

They have lots of stamens with lots of pollen. The wind blows it away.

In spring you may see clouds of pollen blowing off grass flowers. Most of this pollen will be wasted, but some will stick on to the stigmas of the grass flowers.

Wood-Rush flowers

Rye flowers

All trees have flowers. Many trees use the wind to move their pollen.

The Walnut Tree has two kinds of flowers. One kind of flower has a large pistil. The other kind of flower is made of lots of stamens.

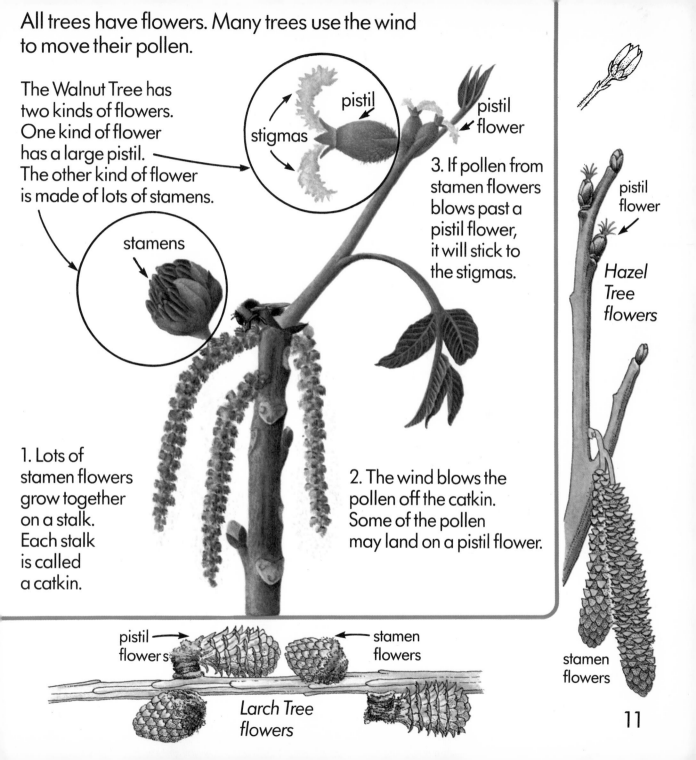

pistil

stigmas

stamens

pistil
flower

3. If pollen from stamen flowers blows past a pistil flower, it will stick to the stigmas.

1. Lots of stamen flowers grow together on a stalk. Each stalk is called a catkin.

2. The wind blows the pollen off the catkin. Some of the pollen may land on a pistil flower.

pistil
flower

Hazel
Tree
flowers

stamen
flowers

pistil
flowers

stamen
flowers

Larch Tree
flowers

11

What happens to the pollen

stigma

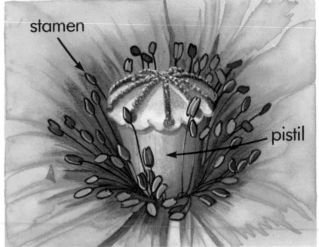

stamen

pistil

1. A bee has left pollen on this stigma. The pollen came from another Poppy flower.

2. Each grain of pollen grows a tube down inside the pistil.
There are ovules inside the pistil.

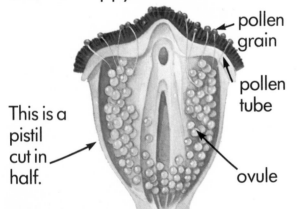

pollen grain

pollen tube

This is a pistil cut in half.

ovule

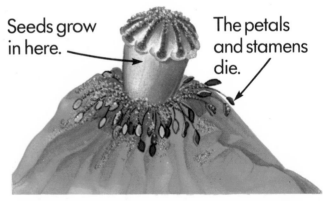

Seeds grow in here.

The petals and stamens die.

3. When a tube reaches an ovule, the inside of the pollen grain moves out of the tube and joins with the ovule.

4. The ovules in the pistil have been fertilized by the pollen.
The fertilized ovules will grow into Poppy seeds.

The flowers on the Poppy plant can be fertilized only when an insect brings pollen from another Poppy plant.

A Poppy flower cannot use its own pollen to fertilize its own ovules. The pollen will not grow tubes down into the pistil.

Poppy pollen will not grow tubes in the Buttercup pistil.

13

More about pollen

Many flowers are like the Poppy. They do not use their own pollen to fertilize themselves. Pollen must be brought from another flower of the same kind by visitors or by the wind.

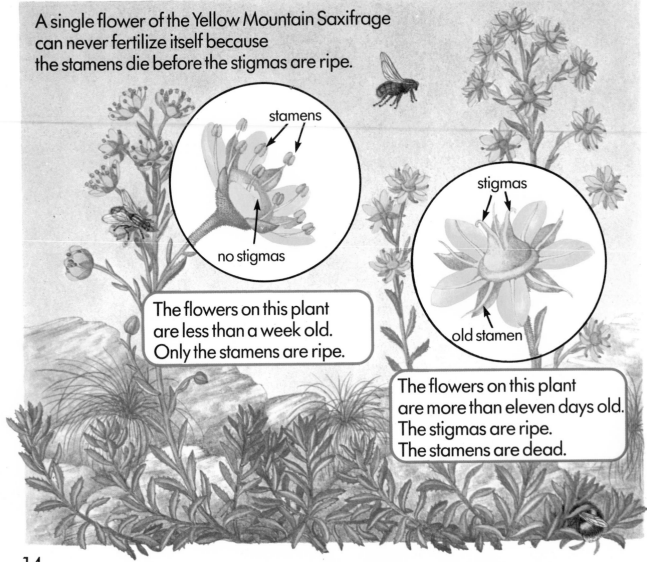

A single flower of the Yellow Mountain Saxifrage can never fertilize itself because the stamens die before the stigmas are ripe.

stamens

no stigmas

The flowers on this plant are less than a week old. Only the stamens are ripe.

stigmas

old stamen

The flowers on this plant are more than eleven days old. The stigmas are ripe. The stamens are dead.

The pollen of this Bee Orchid is moved only by male Eucera Bees. But if no Eucera Bees visit the Orchid it will use its own pollen to fertilize itself.

1. This Bee Orchid looks and smells like a female Eucera Bee. This is how the Orchid attracts male Eucera Bees.

Two sacs of pollen.

2. If a male Bee lands on a flower, the two pollen sacs stick on to his head.

Stigma is in here.

3. This is another male Eucera Bee. He has pollen on his head from another Bee Orchid.

4. As he lands on this flower, the pollen will stick on to the stigma and fertilize the flower.

If no Bees visit this Bee Orchid, it will fertilize itself.

This is how the Bee Orchid fertilizes itself.

The stamens bend over.

The Pollen sacs touch the stigma.

How seeds leave the plant

1. The ovules in this Poppy pistil have been fertilized. They are growing into seeds.

2. The pistil swells. It is now a fruit with seeds inside it.

3. Holes open in the top. When the wind blows the fruit, the seeds fall out.

Looking inside a seed

This is a bean seed. It has a thick skin to protect the parts inside.

This tiny shoot will grow into a new plant.

If you split open a bean seed, this is what you will see inside.

This is a tiny root.

These are two seed leaves full of food. The shoot will use this food when it grows.

When the seeds in the fruits are ripe, the wind or animals may move them away from the plant.

Birds eat fruits and drop the seeds.

Because of their shape, Maple Tree fruits spin to the ground.

The Cranesbill fruit springs open and its seeds fly out.

Sometimes animals bury fruits to eat later. The seeds that do not get eaten may grow.

The wind blows away the Dandelion fruits.

Buttercup fruits may catch on to the fur of animals.

Plants make lots of seeds but only a few of the seeds will grow into new plants. The others die or get eaten.

How a seed grows

1. Autumn
A bird drops a Sunflower seed by accident.

2. Winter
The seed falls to the ground and gets covered over.

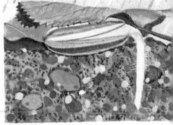

3. Spring
Rain makes the seed swell. A root grows down into the soil.

6. Late spring
The Sunflower plant grows a flower bud. The plant is now taller than a person.

bud

7. Summer
The buds open.

Nasturtium

Pea

Oak acorn

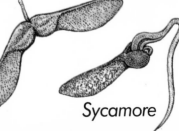

Sycamore

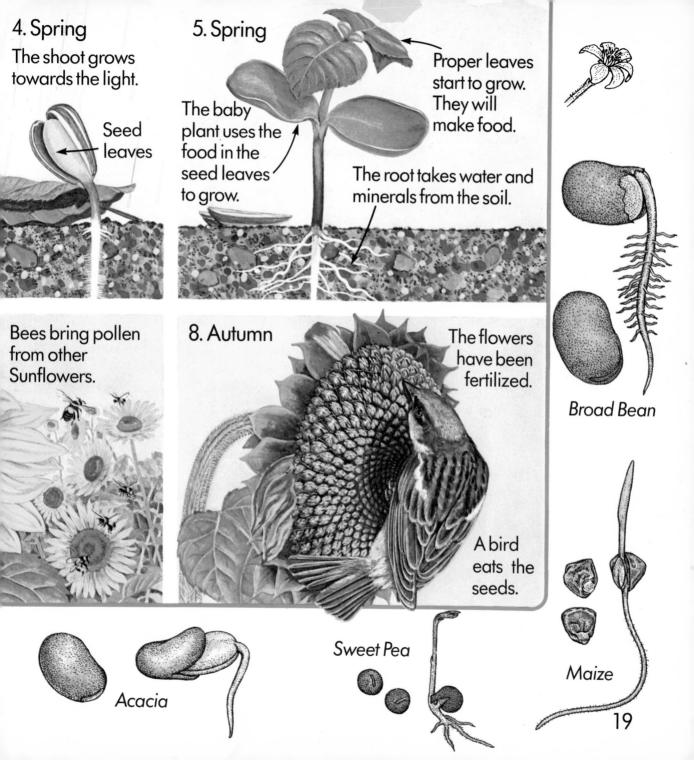

4. Spring

The shoot grows towards the light.

Seed leaves

5. Spring

The baby plant uses the food in the seed leaves to grow.

Proper leaves start to grow. They will make food.

The root takes water and minerals from the soil.

Bees bring pollen from other Sunflowers.

8. Autumn

The flowers have been fertilized.

A bird eats the seeds.

Broad Bean

Acacia

Sweet Pea

Maize

19

How flowers and insects work together

Flowers make most nectar and scent when their pistil or stamens are ripe because this is when they need to attract visitors.

Bees visit these Cherry flowers in the morning. This is when the flowers have most nectar.

New Honeysuckle flowers open in the evening. This is when moths visit them.

The flowers make lots of scent in the evening, but only a little scent in the day.

Bees visit these Apple flowers in the afternoon. This is when the flowers have most nectar.

Many plants take several weeks to open all their flowers. Bees come back to these plants day after day until all the flowers are over.

The Willowherb takes about a month to open all its flowers. The first flowers to open are at the bottom of the stem. The last flowers to open are at the top of the stem.

Willowherb or Fireweed

Horse Chestnut Tree flowers

New flowers open every day.
They have lots of nectar.
Yellow guide-lines point the way to the nectar.

new guide lines

old guide lines

When the nectar is finished, the guide-lines turn red. Bees do not visit old flowers with red guide-lines.

As each flower gets older, it makes more nectar. Bees always visit older Willowherb flowers first.

21

Keeping pollen safe

Most flowers try to keep their pollen safe and dry. Cold weather, rain and dew could damage the pollen or wash it away.

When flowers are closed, the pollen is kept safe.

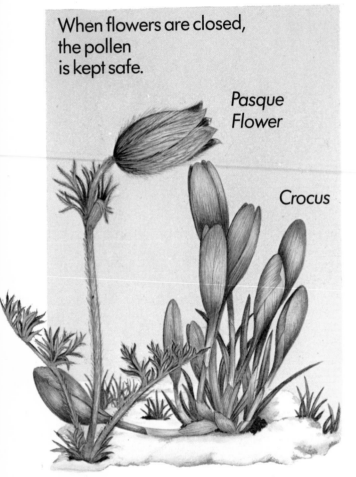

Pasque Flower

Crocus

When flowers are closed, rain and dew cannot get inside.

Ox-eye Daisy

Daisy

These flowers come out in early spring. The flowers open only when it is warm and sunny. If the sun goes in, they close up their petals. The flowers open again when the sun comes out.

These flowers close in the evening and in bad weather. If they have to stay closed for several days, they will fertilize themselves.

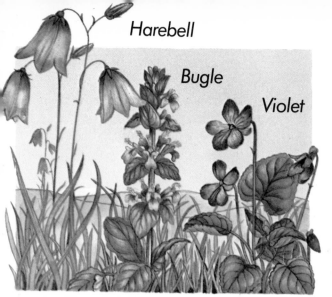

Harebell

Bugle

Violet

These flowers do not need to close their petals to keep pollen safe. Water cannot collect inside them.

Broom

Petals are closed

Petals open when a bee lands.

The stamens and the pistil of the Broom flower are kept safe inside the petals. They spring out when a bee lands on the bottom petals.

stamen has not split

pollen

stamen has split

Ripe stamens of Apple Tree flowers split open to let out the pollen. The stamens will split open only on warm days.

moth

New Catchfly flowers open in the evening. This is when moths visit them. But if the evenings are very cold, no new flowers will open.

23

Picture puzzle

There are nine flowers and nine fruits on this page. Can you guess which fruits belong to which flowers? You can see most of them in this book.

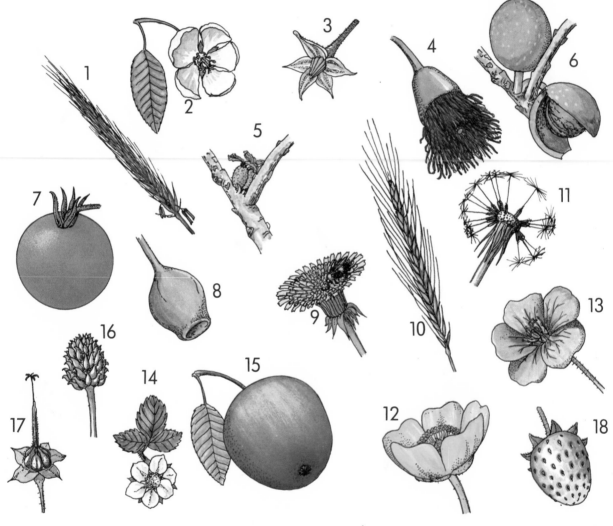

INDEX

FLOWERS